DANDELION MAGIC

Go Ahead, Make Your Wish!

written by
Darren Farrell

illustrated by
Maya Tatsukawa

Dial Books for 🕯 Young Readers

This is Jonah.

Look what he found.

He picked a dandelion!

Can you say "HELLO!" to him?

Jonah's nana thinks dandelions are magical.

She says, "Each year, somewhere in the world, one magical dandelion grows."

One year she found it
and wished for a grandson.

Then...

POOF!

Jonah appeared.

Can you believe that?

Maybe Jonah's dandelion is magical.

Let's see!

Close your eyes.
Take a deep breath.
Make a special wish.
And BLOW!

It worked! It worked!
You turned Jonah into a pineapple!

Wait...

Why did you turn Jonah into a PINEAPPLE??

Well, at least we know
this dandelion is magical!

Try again!

Close your eyes.

Make a special wish.

And
BLOW!

FANTASTIC!
A PIRATE!

Jonah has always wanted to be a pirate.

Hmmm, his boat isn't moving.
Will you blow a great BIG gust of wind
so Jonah can go find the treasure?

Get ready!

Breathe in...

and
BLOW!

Blow THREE more times

REALLY FAST

so Jonah can

REACH

THAT

TREASURE!

AHHHHH!
WATCH OUT FOR THE
SEA SERPENT!

SCARE HIM AWAY
WITH A LOUD NOISE!

ROAR AS LOUD AS YOU CAN!!

Oh good, he's gone.

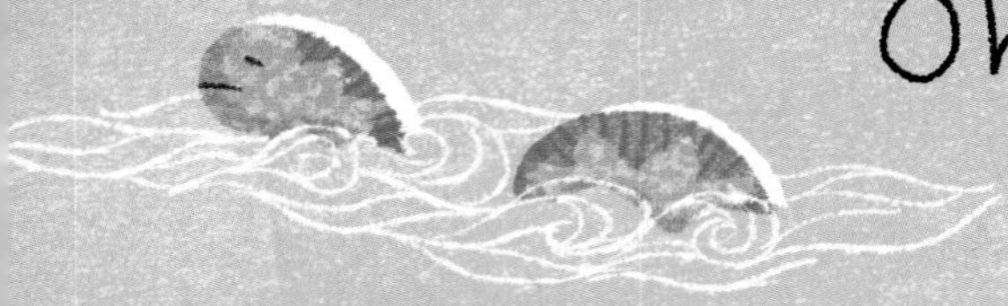

But look out!

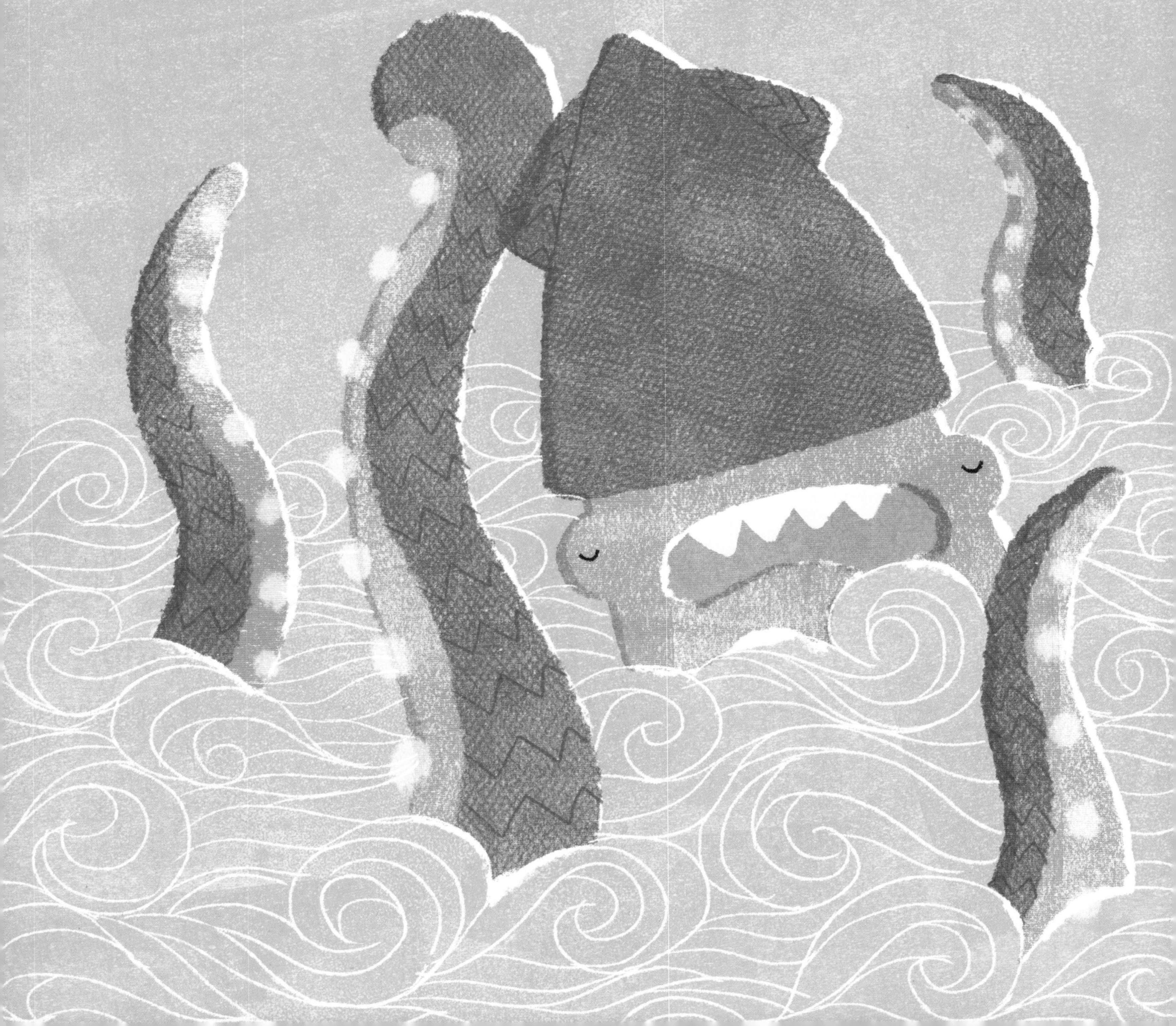

HOLY CHEESE-STRAWS!
IT'S A GIANT SQUID!!

DISTRACT HER!
QUICK, MAKE A SCARY FACE!

Nice work!

I didn't know you could be so scary!!

HEADS UP, HERE COMES
A DRAGON TOO!

WHAT WILL WE DO?

PUT OUT THAT FIRE WITH YOUR WETTEST WET RASPBERRY! STICK OUT YOUR TONGUE AND BLOW WITH ALL YOUR MIGHT!!

UH-OH

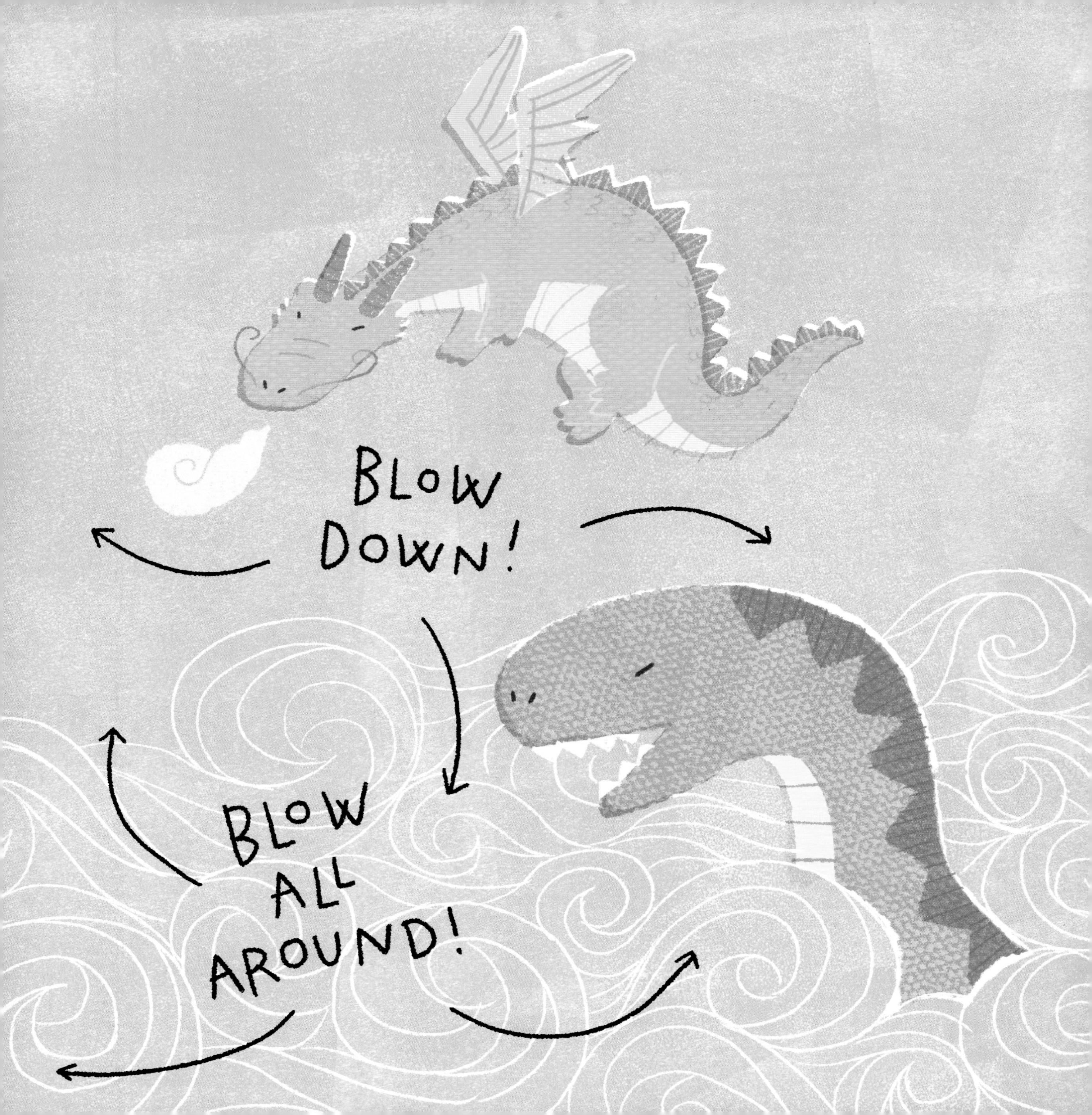

BLOW DOWN!

BLOW ALL AROUND!

Oh no, look what you did.

You started a HURRICANE!

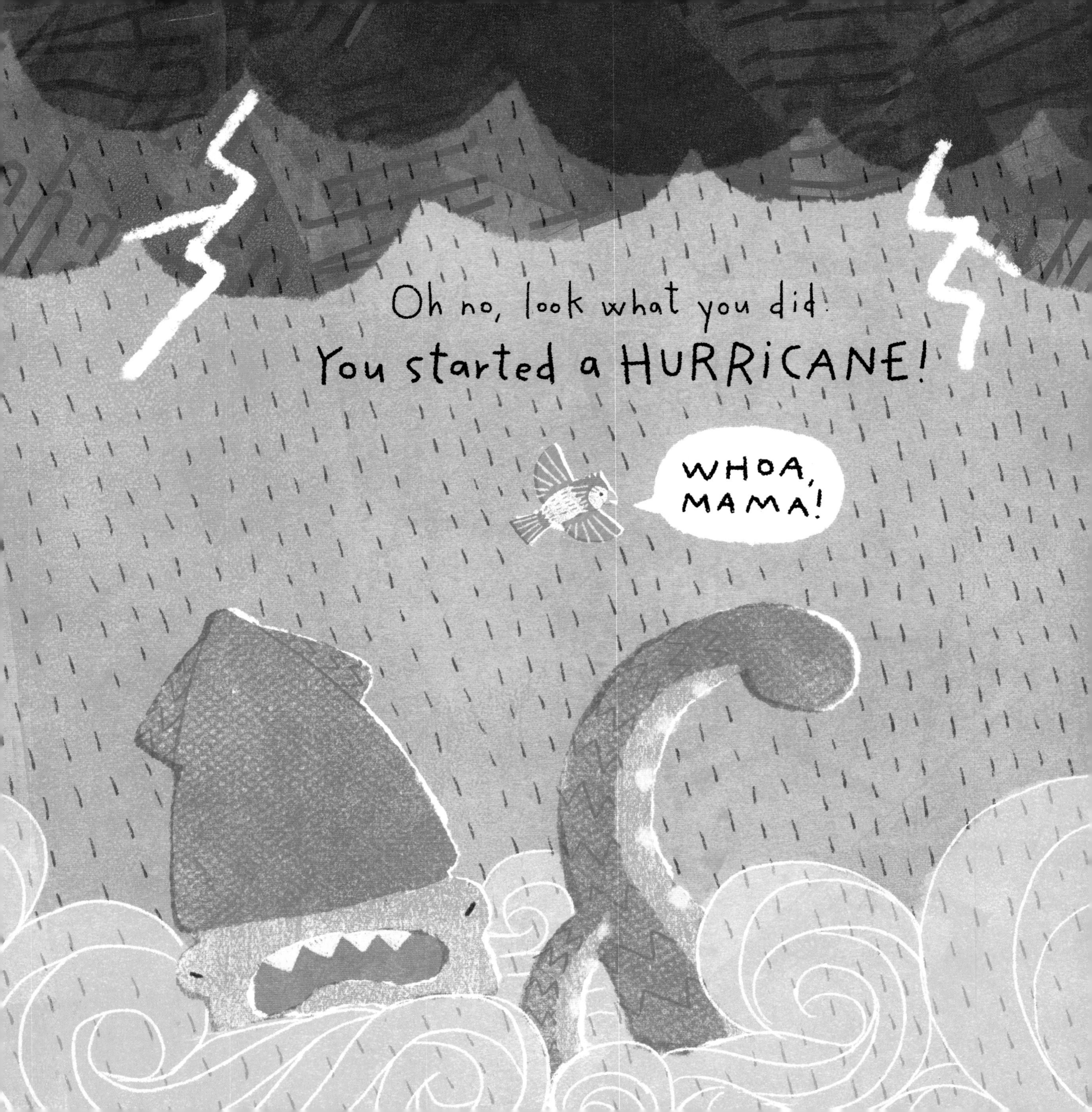

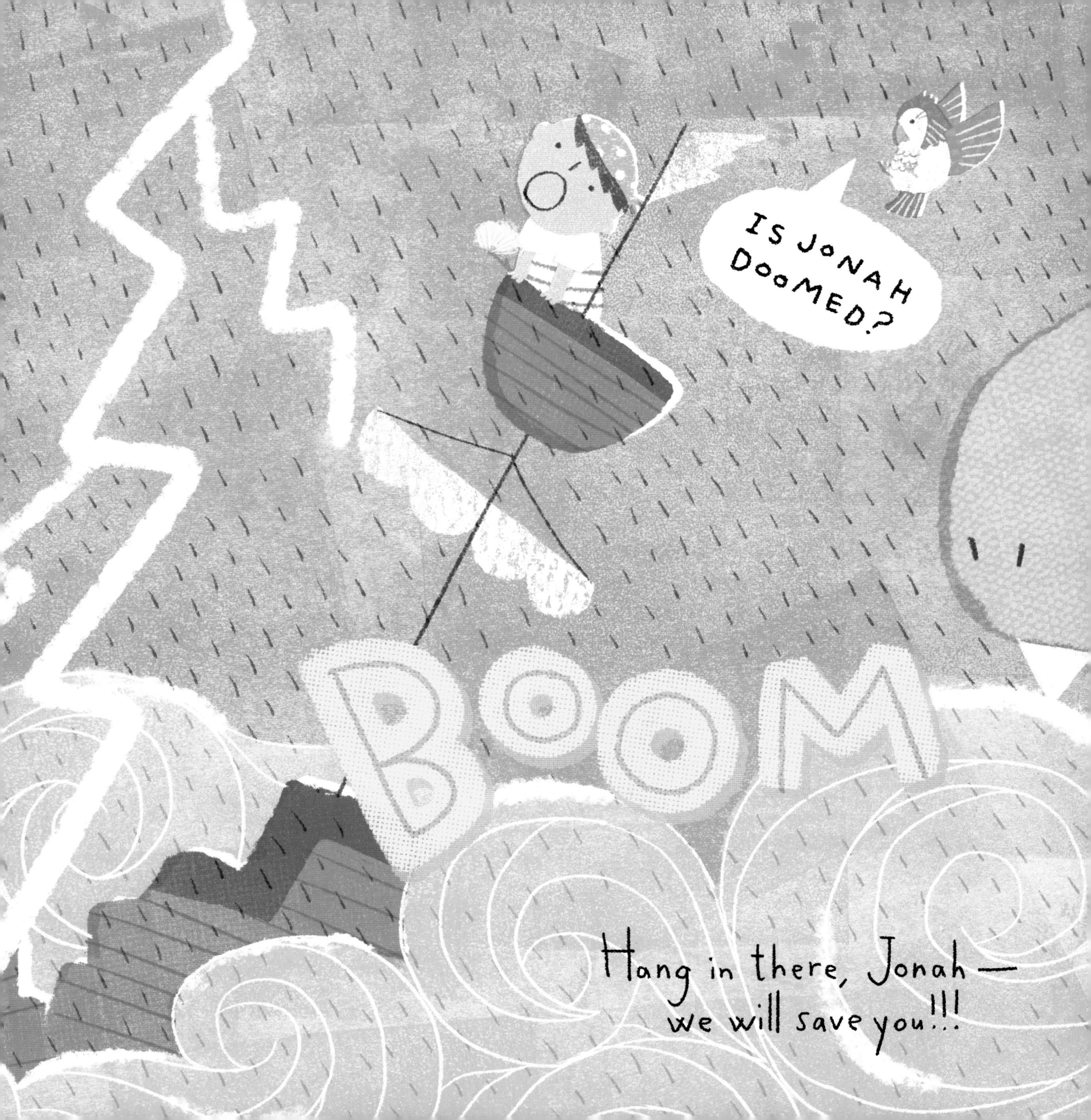

Hang in there, Jonah —
we will save you!!!

Blow hard, and WISH even harder!

A PIZZA? A PIZZA?
You wished for a pizza?

How can you
think about
PIZZA
at a time
like this?

You know, you are very, very
LUCKY!

There is one magic fuzz left.

Make it count.

Save Jonah.

BLOW NOW!

OOOSH

SUPER-NANA
TO THE RESCUE!

You made a great wish!

Phew!
You saved Jonah.
Let's get him home to bed.
What an exciting day!

Please blow the sun away.

Three cheers for a peaceful night.

HURRAH!

YEE-HEE!

Woo-HOO!

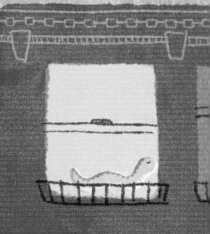

Now blow Jonah
a soft kiss good night.

"Each year,
somewhere in the world,
one magical dandelion grows."

Who will
find it next?

Will it be you?

For Jonah and anyone who
has ever blown on a dandelion.
—D.F.

To my Dial family, for making
my dandelion wishes come true.
—M.T.

DIAL BOOKS FOR YOUNG READERS
An imprint of Penguin Random House LLC, New York

First published in the United States of America by Dial Books for Young Readers,
an imprint of Penguin Random House LLC, 2021

Text copyright © 2021 by Darren Farrell • Illustrations copyright © 2021 by Maya Tatsukawa

Manufactured in China • ISBN 9780593112908
Special Markets ISBN 9780593531143 Not for Resale
1 3 5 7 9 10 8 6 4 2

Design by Jennifer Kelly • Text hand-lettered by Maya Tatsukawa
The artwork was created digitally with handmade textures.

The publisher does not have any control over and does not assume any responsibility
for author or third-party websites or their content.